Green Beans
and Other
Silly Poems

by Nancy Leber and Holli Leber
Illustrated by Tony Griego

SCHOLASTIC INC.
New York   Toronto   London   Auckland   Sydney

Green Beans

Green beans, green beans,
I do not mean to brag.
Little beans, long beans,
I can eat this big, big bag!

Bake them, steam them,
Green beans in a pot.
Grill them, chill them,
I like them iced or hot.

Dip them, heat them,
I eat them for my lunch.
Green beans, green beans,
I like the crunch, crunch, crunch.

I like only green beans,
I can eat a lot.
Fill my plate with green beans,
but please . . . *no peas!*

My Feet

This bug has 100 feet.
(What could they all do?)
All the pets I know have four,
yet I need only two.

But my two feet don't seem to work,
If I want to keep a beat.
That is what Sis means
when she says I have two left feet!

Six Little Sheep

Six little sheep ride to work in a jeep.

Lots of cars go BEEP, BEEP, BEEP.

One little sheep jumps up from her seat.

"We need some speed. This ride is

no treat."

So she hops out and runs down the street.

Five little sheep ride to work in a jeep.

Lots of cars go BEEP, BEEP, BEEP.

One little sheep jumps up from her seat.

"This long ride makes me want to sleep."

So she hops out and runs down the street.

Four little sheep ride to work in a jeep.

Lots of cars go BEEP, BEEP, BEEP.

One little sheep jumps up from her seat.

"I am red as a beet. Get me out of

this heat."

So she hops out and runs down the street

Three little sheep ride to work in a jeep.
Lots of cars go BEEP, BEEP, BEEP.
One little sheep jumps up from her seat.
"This ride is so long I need to eat."
She hops out and runs down the street.

BEEP!

BEEP!

BEEP!

BAA

EP!

BEEP!

BEEP!

Two little sheep ride to work in a jeep.
Lots of cars go BEEP, BEEP, BEEP.
One little sheep jumps up from her seat.
"I must not be late. I will use my feet."
She hops out and rolls down the street.

Only one little sheep rides to work
in a jeep!
CREEP...CREEP...CREEP!

A Little Man Went to Sea

A little man went to sea, sea, sea,
To see what he could see, see, see.
But the only thing he could see, see, see,
was the very, very deep, deep
sea, sea, sea.

The Lost Sock

Little Pete is not so neat.

"I don't know where my sock is!"

He picks up the sheet,

and sees socks on feet,

but not one of the socks is his!

"I don't know where my sock is!"

I Am Only Just a Kid

I am only just a kid.
Who knows what I will be.
I only know that I will work
to be the very best ME.

/e/e	/e/ea	/e/ee	-eat
be	eat	beep	eat
he	beans	beet	beat
me	beat	creep	heat
she	heat	deep	neat
	mean(s)	feet	seat
	neat	green	treat
	peas	jeep	
	please	keep	
	sea	need	
	seat	see(s)	
	steam	seem	
	treat	sheep	
		sheet	
		sleep	
		speed	
		street	
		three	

Phonics Reader 18 ★ Words to Remember

know   little   long   only   work

Phonics Reader 18 ★ Story Words

cars   don't   four   rolls   very

16